Frank Mulligan

Illustrated by Terry Myler

THE CHILDREN'S PRESS

To Teresa

First published 2001 by
The Children's Press
45 Palmerston Road, Dublin 6

2 4 6 8 7 5 3

© Text Frank Mulligan
© Illustrations Terry Myler

ISBN 1 901737 34 9

Typeset by Computertype Limited
Printed by Colour Books Limited

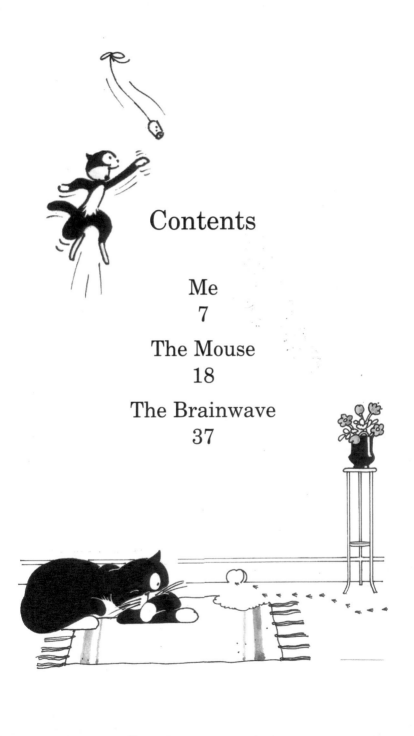

Contents

Me
7

The Mouse
18

The Brainwave
37

1 Me

Once I was called Corky.

Missus Cook (I live with Mister and Missus Cook) told me that when I was a kitten I used to spend all my time playing with a cork.

Must have been mad.

Now that I'm old – I mean older – I have more sense.

No more chasing after corks.

I've better things to do with my life.

Like eating and sleeping.

I've also changed my name to Cookie.

Well, *I* didn't change it.

People who came in used to say, 'How is … what's its name?'

They only asked because they had just fallen over me (I sleep inside the door).

Mrs Cook would say 'Cookie'. Anyway the name stuck.

You could say I'm a lazy cat.

I get up late and take a run in the yard. Well, it's really more of a walk.

When I come in I have a little snack and a big bowl of milk.

I have my own bowl with my name on it.

Cookie

I'm very fond of milk. Good
for the bones, Missus Cook says.
How can she tell?
No one can see my bones.
Or can she?

Then I go to sleep and dream
about dinner.

Dinner is the big meal of the day.

Mr Cook and I can hardly wait for it.

After breakfast he always says, 'What's on the menu?'

Today's Special

Monday — Meat balls

Tuesday — Cod

Wednesday — Stew

Thursday — Rabbit Pie

Friday — Whiting

Saturday — Chicken

Sunday — Roast beef

After dinner I take another nap.

Around five o'clock I go for a stroll in the garden.

See what the story is.

Nibble a bit of grass.

Smell the flowers – if there are any. Mister Cook isn't much of a gardener.

Chat up the cat next door if she's around.

help

When I come in, the fire is lit and I nap out in front of it.

The Cooks sit in chairs each side of the fire and they sleep too.

A little supper.

Then bed.

What a life!

It's one long song.

2 The Mouse

Only one thing bugs me.

There's a mouse in the house.

He has made a few holes in the wall, low down, and is in and out all the time.

Does he think I'm going to hang around all night

He chews up the rug when there's no food around.

The cheek!

It's not much of a rug (between you and me it's seen better days).

But it's *our* rug and that crazy mouse has no business taking bites out of it.

He seems to be a smart kind of mouse.

Missus Cook has set traps for him but he just never gets caught.

Every morning the cheese is gone but where's the mouse?

I don't eat cheese so we all know it must be him.

(Must be costing them a fortune to keep him in cheese.)

Well, it's not my problem.

Anyway, I'm too old to chase after mice.

I'll go to sleep again. Maybe when I wake up he'll be gone.

The sound of voices wakes me.
It's that awful Missus Drip
from next door. With her son.
The drip of all Drips.
Missus Drip is saying in a
very loud voice, 'Do you mean
to say that you haven't got rid
of that mouse yet?'

'We haven't,' says Missus
Cook. She looks at the end of
her rope.

'We've tried and tried. He
eats the cheese but never gets
caught.'

'What you need is a good cat,' shouts Missus Drip.

'But we have a cat,' Mister Cook puts in, in a low voice.

He's afraid of Missus Drip.

'That thing? Call him a cat?'
snarls Missus Drip.

My eyes are shut – well, one
is – but I know that they are
all looking at me.

'Get rid of that cat. Get a new one. A cat that can catch mice.' Why does she have to shout? Hard on the ears.

She's still at it.

'If you don't, the house will be over-run with mice. They'll start coming into *our* house.

'What are you going to do about *THAT*?'

'We'll think about it,' says
Missus Cook. Her voice is low
and sad.

'You do that … or else!'

The Drips go out, with a loud bang of the door.

I have a splitting headache.

'We'll have to do something,' says Mister Cook. His voice is sad too.

Doom and gloom.

I get the message.

Things don't look any better in the morning.

In fact, they look worse.

Much worse.

Unless I look lively, I'll be out on my ear!

Homeless!

No more good meals.
No more warm fires.

I see the future stretch out
before me.

Cold and hunger.

Wet fur. Torn paws.

Empty tum.

It's all so depressing.

I'll think about it tomorrow.

That night I have a terrible
dream.

I'm knocking at the door and
they won't let me in.

It's snowing like mad and
I'm slowly turning into a
snowman.

'Let me in!'
I croak, my
voice weak
with cold
and hunger.
  'Let me in!'

I hear Missus Cook's voice.
'Oh, poor Cookie. We'll have
to let him in.'

'No way,' screams Missus Drip, who won't let her open the door.

'That cat is useless. Get another one.'

The door opens. As I try to crawl in, a blast of cold water hits me.

I turn into an icicle.

When I wake up, I'm in a
cold sweat.

I can hear the Cooks talking.

About the mouse – and me.

I know now that it's the Final
Curtain.

Either that mouse goes.

Or I do.

I'll have to catch him.

Fast!

But how?

3 The Brainwave

I have an idea. I'll make a
better mouse-trap. That's how!
But how?
Hold on a mo. Time to put
the grey cells to work.

I have it!
I'll make a *decoy* trap.

What an idea!

And all my own.

I'll make a model of a Ms Mouse and put her at the end of a bottle.

Then I'll fix up a trap.

With board and string.

When the mouse goes into
the bottle, I pull the string.

The board comes up.

SNAP!

He's caught.

Now for some play
dough...

This is harder than I thought
… she doesn't look good enough
to me… hope he, the mouse, has
poor eyesight… give her a bit
more colour… a bow
in her hair.

Now I'll push her into the
bottle… now for the string with
the piece of wood attached…

Now, where will I put the
bottle?

Over there?

No, on the way to the fridge
– good thinking – I'll leave the
fridge door open tonight...

Yawn, yawn.

Time for some old shut-eye.

No doubt about it.

Thinking is very, very, *very* exhausting.

I wake to hear the patter of little feet.

My mouse!

I open an eye.

He sees Ms Mouse, sidles into the bottle...

I pull the string… and…
SNAP!
He's caught!
How's that for sheer
brain power!

'Now Mister Mouse,' I say to him. 'What am I to do with you?'

'Oh, please, let me live,' says the mouse. 'If you don't, my family will starve.

'Have a heart!'

'Family? You mean there are more of you?'

'Yes. There's me and my four, poor, motherless kids to bring up in this world.

'Four kids? That's a handful to be landed with.

'What happened your wife?'

The little mouse begins to sob.

When he can speak again, he says sadly, 'In the last house I lived in, there was this young, strong, fast cat.

'He caught my wife one night and that was the end. So we moved here.'

He falls to his knees and clasps his paws.

'Please let me go,' he sobs.

By this time the four kids have come out of the mouse hole.

They're all sobbing and bawling.

They make such a row we'll have the Cooks down pronto.

Now I must say I was cross
when the mouse talked about
the cat who killed his wife.
   Big? Strong? Fast?
   What am I?
   Small? Weak? Slow?

'I may not be as young as I was,' I say to him. 'Who is?

'But I have brains which is more than you have.

'Don't you know a mouse should never come into a house where there is a cat?'

'I know,' says the mouse, 'but what was I do do? I was at my wits' end.

'One of the kids had a racking cough and another had a drag in his leg.'

'Please let me go,' says the
mouse again. 'The kids and I
will pack our bags and move
out... honest... *don't kill me.*'

At this, the kids all start
bawling and wailing again.

Now, what was *I* to do?

My computer!

Click on 'Shortcut to brainbox'.

Click on 'Overdrive'.

Super! Idea! Ideas! Ideas!

I choose the option: *Make him an offer; he can't refuse*,

I say, 'I don't want to kill you, I'm not into blood sports.

'But if I do let you go, you must do something for me.'

'Anything! Anything!' says the mouse. 'Just say the word...'

'It's very simple. When you leave here you must tell every mouse you meet that in this house lives the BIGGEST, the **youngest,** the **STRONGEST,** the *fastest* cat in the world.'

'I will, I will,' says the mouse. 'I'll start with all the relations living on this road. All four hundred and five of them.'

I give them a hunk of cheese to help them on their way.

They all disappear.

The whole five of them.

Pronto.

To this day mice have never re-entered my home.

The Cooks are delighted.

The Drips are raging mad.
Now they have mice that
they can't catch.

Well, that's their problem!

Here the meals just keep
getting better and better.

Only now I have
another problem.

Can I be getting fatter?

I know I'm not getting any
thinner.